"Look, Salem! He's a mascot, just like you!"

Sabrina leaned over Salem to see the photo of a fat bulldog. He was wearing a sweater and holding a pennant in his paws.

"What do you mean, just like me?" asked the cat suspiciously. "You mean other pets are doing this mascot stuff? I thought I had this racket to myself."

"Well, this one is," Sabrina said. "He's the mascot at a big college, and you're only the mascot at a high school."

Salem hissed again. "This . . . this . . . *dog* has a better job than I do?"

"Sure, he does. Their games are on TV, and he gets to travel all over the country."

"I want his job," declared Salem.

She took another look at the photo of the grizzled bulldog. "I wouldn't count on getting this dog's job. He doesn't look like he wants to go anywhere."

"We'll see," answered Salem, swishing his tail.

Sabrina, the Teenage Witch™
Salem's Tails™

Available from MINSTREL Books

New York   London   Toronto   Sydney   Singapore

This book is a work of fiction. Names, characters, places and incidents
are products of the author's imagination or are used fictitiously. Any
resemblance to actual events or locales or persons living or dead is
entirely coincidental.

A MINSTREL PAPERBACK *Original*

 A Minstrel Book published by
POCKET BOOKS, a division of Simon & Schuster, Inc.
1230 Avenue of the Americas, New York, NY 10020

Salem quotes taken from the following episodes:
"Whose So-Called Life Is It, Anyway?" written by Charlie Tercek
"Little Orphan Hilda" written by Nick Bakay

ISBN: 0-671-03837-0

First Minstrel Books printing September 2000

10 9 8 7 6 5 4 3 2 1

A MINSTREL BOOK and colophon are registered trademarks of
Simon & Schuster, Inc.

SABRINA THE TEENAGE WITCH and all related titles, logos
and characters are trademarks of Archie Comics Publications, Inc.

Cover photo by Pat Hill Studio

Printed in the U.S.A.

For Eric, the football player

"Relax, Salem, you can always fall back on your skills as an entertainer. . . . I'm going to starve."

—*Salem*

Chapter 1

"Cream him! Smash him!" yelled Salem Saberhagen. He was sitting on the couch, and he began to jump around like a kitty on hot cement. "Stomp his face!"

Sabrina Spellman strolled through the living room, and she glanced at the black cat. She didn't think it was strange that the cat was yelling—after all, she was half-witch herself—but she wondered what he was yelling about.

1

"Are you looking at a picture of Drell again?"

Drell was the head of the Witches' Council, the one who had turned Salem from a warlock into a cat for trying to take over the world. Salem could still talk, but he couldn't do magic anymore. He had never forgiven Drell or any of the witches on the council for giving him fur.

"No," said Salem, "I'm watching a football game on TV." His tail swished excitedly. "Hold them, you morons! Don't let those idiots score!"

Sabrina stopped and looked quizzically at the TV. "Is it really the Morons playing the Idiots?"

"That's what I call them," answered Salem. "The Idiots are winning, but I bet ten dollars on the Morons. Hold that line!"

"I didn't know you liked football." Sabrina sat on the couch beside her cat.

"I didn't know I liked it, either,"

2

answered the cat, "until I started watching. Football is a lot like war, and I love war. You have big men in armor crashing into each other. It reminds me of the Middle Ages."

"And you loved the Middle Ages," said Sabrina. "War, poverty, disease, no plumbing."

"Ah, yes, those were the good old days," answered Salem wistfully. "But football is almost as good. Hey, look! It's my favorite part—the mad charge into enemy lines!"

"I think it's called a kickoff," said Sabrina.

Salem swished his tail happily as he watched the melee. "Sabrina, doesn't your high school have a football team?"

"Yes, we have a football team," she answered. "Harvey is on the team, and he plays more often since he scored a touchdown. But I wouldn't bet on them,

because the Fighting Scallions hardly ever win."

"Scallions? Your football team is named after a vegetable?"

"Yes," answered Sabrina. "They were supposed to be the Fighting *Stallions,* but there was a mistake on the T-shirts. Now we're the Fighting Scallions."

"Why don't you take me to a football game?" asked Salem excitedly. "I would love to see all this mayhem in person."

"Um, people don't usually take their cats to football games."

"I don't know why not," said Salem. "Cats love to see people running around and acting crazy."

"Well, I'm sorry, I can't take you to a football game. I don't think they allow animals in the stadium."

"When is the next game?" asked Salem innocently.

"This Friday night we have a home

game, but you can't go." Sabrina rose to her feet and headed for the kitchen. "Just catch the highlights on the news."

"But than I'd miss the best parts," muttered Salem. After Sabrina left the room, he added, "I'm going to that football game on Friday night, whether *you* like it or not."

Salem didn't say anything else about football the whole week. On Friday after school the cat noticed that Sabrina was making sandwiches and packing them into a picnic basket. He always watched when people were in the kitchen, but this was more interesting than usual.

"Going on a picnic?" he asked innocently.

"It's for the game tonight," she answered. She stopped and looked at him. "You don't want to go to the football game still, do you?"

"A cat go to a football game?" he scoffed. "How silly!"

She laughed, too. "Yes, it is silly. Here, have a piece of chicken."

Salem wasn't going to turn *that* down, and he gobbled the treat. He noticed Sabrina's boots, mittens, and thermal winter coat. "Expect to be cold, do you?"

She shrugged. "It's not a real football game unless you're suffering from frost-bite."

"That's not for me," answered Salem with a shiver. "I only watch sports on TV. If there's no football, I'll watch wrestling. Or bowling."

"Smart cat." Sabrina opened up the refrigerator and took out a plate full of deviled eggs. Carefully she wrapped the eggs and packed them in the picnic bas-ket.

Mmmm, thought Salem, *I love deviled eggs*.

6

"Aunt Hilda and Aunt Zelda are going to a party in the Other Realm tonight," said the teenage witch. "And Dreama is going to the game with me. You'll be all alone here. Are you sure you won't be bored?"

"Oh, no," answered the cat. "I'm going out for dinner myself in just a few minutes. There's a new fish restaurant on State Street, and I want to check out their garbage cans."

"You be careful," warned Sabrina.

"Aren't I always?"

Sabrina frowned at that statement. She checked her watch and gasped. "Uh-oh! My friends will be here to pick us up any minute. I'd better tell Dreama to hurry up."

Dreama was a witch from the Other Realm who was hanging out with Sabrina to learn how to live with mortals. *Just what we needed*, thought Salem, two *teenage witches*.

7

Sabrina hurried out of the kitchen, leaving him alone with the picnic basket. It was a big wooden basket with two large flaps. There were latches on the flaps, but Sabrina had forgotten to close them.

"Hmmm," said the cat to himself, "I *am* going out to dinner tonight—that much is true. But it won't be at the fish restaurant."

Looking around to make sure no one was watching, Salem opened up one of the big flaps. Mmmm, it smelled delicious inside the basket with all those sandwiches and deviled eggs. And there was just enough room for a kitty to curl up at the bottom and make himself at home.

There will be even more room, thought Salem, *after I eat a few of those eggs.*

Chapter 2

"**B**urp!"

The loud belch came from behind Sabrina. Or was it in front of her? Maybe beside her? It was hard to tell in the crowded bleachers at the Westbridge High football game. Everyone was yelling and talking. Her picnic basket was at her feet, and she had to make sure no one kicked it over.

Lots of fans were eating hot dogs and drinking sodas, so some burps were to be expected. But she kept hearing these loud

9

burps coming from somewhere nearby. Sabrina looked and looked, trying to figure out who was making the rude eruptions.

She stared angrily at the boy right behind her, thinking it had to be *him*. He gave her a goofy smile, as if he thought she was flirting with him. She quickly turned around.

Maybe I shouldn't blame them for eating, thought Sabrina. The game had just started, but it was already lousy. The visiting team, the Sunnyside Badgers, won the coin toss, and it was all downhill from there. The Fighting Scallions kicked off to the Badgers, and now the Badgers were driving easily toward the goal line.

"That's another ten-yard gain," said the weary announcer over the speaker system. "And another first down for the Badgers, who have the ball on the Scallions' eighteen-yard line."

"Push 'em back! Push 'em back! Wa-a-

a-y back!" yelled the Westbridge cheer-leaders.

Their mascot, a guy in a scallion costume, kept jumping around and waving at the crowd. He was trying to get people to cheer for the team. But it was hard to get excited at the sight of a dancing vegetable. *He looks more like a stalk of celery than a scallion,* Sabrina thought.

She looked down at the picnic basket at her feet. She wanted to make sure not to kick the basket, or it would fall through the opening under the seats. They were high up in the bleachers, and the ground was a long way down. It looked as if there was a lot of trash down there under the bleachers.

She wanted to wait until halftime to eat, but this game was so boring that she thought maybe they should go ahead and eat. Dreama and all her friends were talking, not watching the game. Sabrina could see Harvey on the field—bent over

and panting. He had made a couple of tackles, but they were all far downfield. With every play the Badgers moved the ball closer to the goal line.

"Burp!"

There—she heard it again! Sabrina whirled around and glanced at the spectators nearest her. None of them looked guilty of making that big belch. Certainly her friends hadn't done it. *Then where had it come from?*

Inside the picnic basket, Salem rolled around in the empty wrappers and bread crumbs. He tried to get comfortable, but he looked and felt like a plump black pillow. He sniffed around the bottom of the basket, looking for more food, then realized he had eaten it *all.* No wonder he had a stomachache! The last time he had eaten this much, he'd taken a nap and woken up tied to the floor by magical mice.

Salem heard the announcer's voice on the speakers. "That was a hard tackle by Crenshaw. Too bad it was on the five-yard line. That's another first down for the Sunnyside Badgers!"

The Westbridge team was getting creamed, and he was missing it! Now that he had eaten all the food, it was time to watch the game. It was also time to escape before Sabrina found out all the food was gone. The problem was, how could he get out of the basket?

The cat couldn't see anything through the basket, so he didn't know where they were sitting. He didn't even know what the stadium looked like. But he knew he had to get out of that basket before Sabrina discovered him.

Salem decided to poke his head out of the flap and look around. But he didn't realize how fat he had gotten from all that eating. When he climbed up the side

of the basket, his weight caused the basket to tip over.

The basket tipped all the way over and fell through the space under the seats! Salem tumbled from the flap and plunged into the darkness, his legs swinging like windmills. He bounced off a beam and howled like an alleycat as he plummeted downward.

Cats don't always land on their feet, and Salem landed on his head in a pile of trash. He popped up with a paper bag stuck on his head. Scared and confused, the poor cat didn't know where he was! He jumped out of the pile and ran for his life, the paper bag flapping.

Chapter 3

On the football field Harvey was so tired he could barely breathe. He looked at the Sunnyside players coming out of their huddle, and he knew they would score a touchdown. In fact, they would probably score a lot of touchdowns tonight.

"Come on, guys!" he said to his teammates. "Let's hold them!"

His friend Brad sighed and shook his head. His tired eyes seemed to say: *We couldn't hold them if we had a net!*

Both Brad and Harvey were defensive backs, and they were sure on their backs a lot.

Suddenly there was a commotion and laughter in the stands. Harvey turned to see a black cat come running onto the football field. That was funny enough, but the cat had a bag over his head and didn't know where he was going.

Harvey could only see the cat's rear end, but it looked kind of like Salem. He dashed under the goalposts and then ran right in front of the visiting players. They all jumped back in alarm.

"Hey, that's going to be bad luck on them!" said Brad, laughing.

The referees blew their whistles to stop the game, but the loud whistles made the cat go even crazier. He dashed to the side-lines and ran between the legs of the cheer-leaders, causing them all to scream and panic.

This scared the cat even more, and he jumped on the back of the mascot. When his claws sunk in, the poor guy in the scallion costume screeched and tried to run away. But he stumbled and went crashing into the marching band. His head ended up inside a big tuba, and the cat flew off and landed on a lemonade stand.

By now Harvey and all the football players were laughing and slapping their thighs. It was the funniest thing they had ever seen during a football game. Everyone in the stands was laughing, too, and they forgot that they were getting beaten.

When the referees and the coaches started chasing the cat, it got even funnier. He dashed across the field again and leaped onto the visitors' bench. The cat ran the length of the bench, and all the Badger football players scrambled to get out of the way. A bunch of them crashed

into each other and ended up in a big pile.

Now Harvey and the Westbridge team were really laughing. The quarterback of the other team glared at them. "You let that cat onto the field just to delay the game!" he shouted.

"Yeah, you're right!" yelled Harvey. "We let the cat out of the bag!" All the Westbridge players hooted with laughter, making the Badgers even angrier.

A blur ran past Harvey, and he looked up to see a familiar face in a heavy coat. "Sabrina! What are you doing?"

"That's my stupid cat!" she shouted as she ran past the players. Sabrina chased the cat off the field into the parking lot.

The Westbridge players finally stopped laughing, but now they were relaxed. They had also gotten a chance to catch their breath and rest for a couple of minutes. Harvey felt a lot better.

"Hey, what do you say we really hold them this time?" he shouted.

"Yeah!" cried his teammates. "Don't let them score! Push 'em back!"

Football is a funny game, and it depends a lot on emotions. The Fighting Scallions were relaxed and in a good mood on the next play, but the Badgers were angry and uptight. They hiked the ball, but the quarterback forgot to hold on to it.

"Fumble! Fumble!" shouted the announcer. "Who has the ball?"

The referees sorted through a huge pile of players on the goal line. They finally pointed their hands in the other direction, and Harvey jumped from the pile with the ball in his hands.

The announcer shouted happily, "The Fighting Scallions have recovered the ball on the one-yard line! They hold the Badgers for no points!"

19

The Westbridge cheerleaders screamed and jumped around like crazy. The mascot in the vegetable costume was injured, but he waved his hands from the stretcher as they carried him off the field.

Out of sight behind the bleachers, Sabrina scolded Salem. "I can't believe you did that! It's bad enough that you hide in my picnic basket and eat all the food. But then you sneak into the game and make a spectacle of yourself. If five thousand people hadn't been watching you, I would have turned *you* into a ham sandwich!"

"I just wanted to watch a football game in person," pleaded Salem. "Hear the roar of the crowd and watch mortals cream each other! The food was just an extra bonus."

"I'll give you an extra bonus!" snapped Sabrina. She leveled her finger at the cat

and was about to zap him when they heard the crowd roar. That was followed by a huge cheer.

"Something good must have happened for Westbridge," said Salem in amazement.

From a distance they heard the announcer's voice. "It's a touchdown for the Fighting Scallions on a long pass from Kelly to Stinett! The score is Westbridge six, Sunnyside nothing."

They rushed back into the stadium and watched the rest of the game. Nobody complained about Salem being there, and Sabrina pointed at the basket and zapped it with a bolt of magic. Now it was full of sandwiches and deviled eggs again.

It was a fun game to watch, because the Fighting Scallions won 24–7. That was the first time they had beaten the Badgers in four years.

After the game Sabrina held Salem and waited for Harvey to come out of the locker room. They were very surprised when he walked out with Mr. Kraft, the principal. Mr. Kraft didn't usually hang with the students, but he and Harvey were laughing and slapping each other on the back like old friends.

"Ah," said Salem happily, "there's nothing like winning a war! I mean . . . a football game."

"You keep quiet," whispered Sabrina. "You're lucky you're not in more trouble."

"Sabrina!" called Harvey, waving to her. Mr. Kraft, Harvey, and half the team rushed over to her.

"Great game!" said Sabrina, but everybody ignored her. They were all looking at Salem.

Harvey rubbed the cat's head. "Hey, Salem, that was really cool when you ran out on the field. It got us all relaxed, and

we *rocked* after that! We talked to Mr. Kraft, and he says it's okay if you become our new mascot!"

Mr. Kraft shrugged. "Nobody liked the dancing vegetable anyway."

"You'll be good luck for us!" said Brad. Everyone on the team shouted in agreement.

Salem swished his tail and smiled at Sabrina. Not only wasn't the cat in trouble— he was a hero!

With everyone looking at her, all of them so happy, how could Sabrina say no? They had no idea what they were doing by making Salem their mascot. He would probably end up coaching the team!

"All right," she muttered. Harvey grabbed Salem out of her hands and began to pet him. His teammates crowded around, all wanting to pet and coo over their new mascot.

23

"Hey, let's buy him a hot dog!" said Harvey.

"Yeah! Yeah!" agreed everyone. "And some potato chips!"

Sabrina just rolled her eyes. She didn't know how this was going to end, but it wouldn't be good.

Chapter 4

Sabrina stood in the hallway of her high school, and she couldn't believe what she saw. Here came Salem, wearing sunglasses, a white scarf, sitting on a green pillow, being carried by the football team. Green and white were the school colors, and the players held the cat as if he were a precious jewel.

As they passed through the hall, other students bowed down and waved to Salem. *Okay,* thought Sabrina, *so the football team has just won their third*

game in a row. Three games is more than they usually win all season. But Salem doesn't do anything—it's the team that's winning the games.

"All hail our mascot!" yelled a big football player.

"Hail, Salem!" screamed a bunch of girls. They giggled and pointed their fingers at the cat as he passed by on his regal pillow. Salem looked down at Sabrina and stuck his nose in the air.

"Rah! Rah! Kitty!" screamed one of the girls. She saw Sabrina looking at her, and she ran over and gushed, "You don't know us, but we really love your cat! Can we come to his house and visit him sometime? We'll bring him caviar."

Sabrina sniffed. "Why doesn't he just move in with you?"

"Could he?" she squealed, jumping up and down.

"I'm going to be nice to you and say

26

no," replied Sabrina. She tried to get away, but the girls surrounded her.

"Can we sit close to him at the pep rally?" asked one of them.

Sabrina shrugged. "Sure."

They squealed in unison and rushed off. Sabrina could only shake her head at the craziness of it.

She wandered down the hall, ignoring all the happy chatter about the football team. Sabrina was glad the team was winning, and she didn't want to do anything to stop that. But it made her nervous to see Salem getting so much attention. When it came to power and glamour, he never knew when to stop.

"Miss Spellman!" barked a voice behind her, sending a shiver down her spine.

She turned around to see Mr. Kraft headed her way. He looked grumpy and harried as usual, and he peered at her through his thick glasses. "I've got something for you."

The principal reached into his pocket and pulled out a stack of small papers. Sabrina was scared that they were detention slips, because that's what they looked like. He stuffed them into her hand. "Here you go, Miss Spellman."

"But I didn't do anything!"

"Look at them, please."

Shuddering, Sabrina looked at the pages, then she shrieked with delight. "Hall passes! Eight of them   enough to keep me out of all my classes. Thanks a lot, Mr. Kraft! What can I get you from the mall?"

"You're not going to the mall," said the principal tersely. "Salem has a full schedule today, and he needs an assistant. I think you would be perfect for the job."

"Assistant to the mascot?" asked Sabrina, stifling a laugh. "What exactly is Salem doing?"

Kraft pulled a long sheet out of his other pocket and began to read. "First

comes his shampoo and manicure—to get him ready for his video shoot."

"Video shoot?" asked Sabrina with disgust.

"Then at one o'clock Salem is going to appear at Pet Palace for their grand opening. The mayor will introduce him. Just make sure you get back to school in time for the big pep rally." He stuffed the sheet of paper into her other hand.

"Excuse me," said Sabrina, "but I thought I was here to get an education. I'm really longing to go to algebra."

"And you'll need to get around town," said Kraft, ignoring her. He dug deeply into his pants pockets. "Here are some bus tokens."

"Oh, thanks," muttered Sabrina. "Won't they let our famous mascot ride the bus for free?"

"If they do, bring me back the change." Mr. Kraft walked off, chuckling to him-

self. "And you thought you were going to the mall!"

In the dressing room Salem relaxed in a makeup chair while two beauticians combed his shiny black fur. They squirted perfume on him, put powder on his nose, and brushed his whiskers. The cat closed his eyes and purred contentedly, while Sabrina sat in her chair and tried not to be sick.

The beauticians pampered Salem for an hour before they were satisfied. They took some instant photos, and he signed them with his paw print. After they left the room, Salem turned to Sabrina and said, "Remind me to get some photos of myself. We could sell them to my fans."

Sabrina rolled her eyes. "Yes, Master."

The cat turned his attention to a plate of snacks. "Excuse me, Assistant, will you take one of those liver bits and put it in my mouth?"

"Can't you get it?" grumbled Sabrina. "It's only ten inches away from you."

Salem sniffed. "No, I can't. My nails are drying."

The dressing room door opened, and a man with a clipboard stuck his head in. "Salem is wanted on the set."

"It's about time," said Sabrina. She stood up and motioned to the door. "Come on, Salem, let's go."

The cat didn't move a muscle. He just sat there and looked bored. Finally he gazed at his silk pillow, then he looked pointedly at Sabrina.

Sabrina shook her head. "No way am I—"

The man in the doorway scowled at her. "Put him on his pillow, will you! He *is* the star. Boy, good help is hard to find."

Salem gave a loud sigh, as if he couldn't agree more. The man stamped

31

his foot impatiently, until Sabrina picked up the cat, put him on his pillow, and carried him to the stage. "You're pushing it," she whispered to Salem.

Ten minutes later Salem was surrounded by dancing girls dressed as cheerleaders. *They couldn't bother to use real cheerleaders*, thought Sabrina.

The director called "Action!" and they turned on smoke machines, laser beams, and disco lights. Cameras moved in, and loud music thumped throughout the soundstage. The dancers gyrated all around Salem, while the cat did nothing but lick his fur. Then he rolled onto his back. At one point he tried to look menacing.

"Cut!" yelled the director. "That was *wonderful!* Such realism! Such pathos for the common cat!"

Salem swished his tail smugly, while Sabrina rolled her eyes and groaned.

*　　*　　*

Hundreds of people were gathered in the parking lot of the new pet store, Pet Palace. It was the grand opening. Banners were flying, music was playing, and they were giving away prizes and treats. Most of the people in the audience had their dogs, cats, and other pets with them. On the stage a fat man in a blue suit was talking and sweating.

"When I was elected mayor twelve years ago, Westbridge only had *one* pet store," said the man glumly. Then he smiled. "Now it has *two*! This is a great day for our city, because we never want to neglect our four-footed friends. I *love* animals!"

There was a smattering of applause, and the rotund mayor waved and smiled as if everyone loved him. Sabrina yawned and tried to stay awake. It was hard, because she had been rushing

33

around all day, taking Salem here and there. Plus it was hot standing outside in a parking lot in the midday sun. On top of that, Sabrina hadn't had time to eat any lunch.

"Now," said the mayor with a broad smile, "let me introduce another celebrity. There's no doubt that he belongs here, because he *is* one of our favorite pets. Here he is—the undefeated mascot of Westbridge High School—Salem!"

Sabrina started to applaud along with everyone else, because this meant they would be leaving soon. She looked down at the pillow where Salem was sitting. At least he was *supposed* to be sitting there, but the black cat was gone. He was nowhere to be seen.

Nervously the mayor tugged at his collar and motioned toward Sabrina. "I said . . . 'and here's Salem!' "

"He's around here . . . somewhere!"

answered Sabrina with a flustered smile. She wanted to make herself disappear, but everybody was staring at her.

Suddenly there came a horrible shriek from inside the pet store. Sabrina was already on her toes, so she led the charge into the store. The first thing she saw was a huge commotion around the fish tanks. Two clerks were screaming and swinging brooms at a dark shape scurrying between the tanks.

"That lionfish is priceless!" shouted one of them.

A flash of dark fur burst from underneath the tanks and dashed toward the back door. Sabrina quickly saw that it was Salem, with something hanging from his mouth. It was a striped tail, which whipped back and forth, slapping Salem in the face.

Since no one was watching her, Sabrina leveled her finger and zapped the cat. A

35

moment later both Salem and the fish were back in the fish tank, and one of the clerks screamed loudly and fainted. Salem floundered around in the tank, half-drowning and half trying to catch the lionfish.

Sabrina acted fast. She strode toward the fish tank and grabbed the cat by the scruff of the neck. "Excuse me, I'm his assistant." She yanked the cat out and held him dripping over the floor, like a clump of wet laundry. Salem twisted in her grip, trying to get away, but Sabrina held him tightly.

"Oh, Salem, you're such a joker!" she gushed. "Come on, your fans are waiting."

Sabrina marched outside and stuck the wet cat into the mayor's arms. He held the dripping animal at arm's length and grimaced with disgust. "Yuck! I hate cats!"

With that he hurled the cat into the

crowd, and several people screamed in alarm. All the dogs barked insanely, straining at their leashes, and people booed the mayor. It looked as if there might be a riot. Salem sat in the middle of the commotion, shivering and pathetic. Sabrina took pity on him. He hadn't asked to be a mascot—he was drafted into it.

"Sorry, folks!" she said, scooping up the cat. "That's all we have time for today. Salem enjoyed the pet store, I can tell you!"

Sabrina ran across the parking lot, barging through the crowd. As she ran, she popped a spell to dry the dripping cat and her clothes, but that didn't help the situation much. People were still yelling and chasing after them.

"I'm a hit wherever I go!" bragged Salem. "See, they hate to see me leave!"

"Next time I won't rescue you!"

37

vowed Sabrina. She rounded the corner and dashed down an alley. The instant they were alone, she twirled her finger and whisked them away in a swirl of magic.

They popped to safety in a broom closet back at the high school, and Sabrina bumped into a mop and a bucket in the dark. She found the light switch and turned it on, then she finally took time to breathe.

The teenager rubbed her stomach and looked at Salem. "Maybe now I can get some lunch. Unlike you, I haven't spent all day eating."

"Yeah," said Salem with delight. "Is this a great job, or what!"

Sabrina opened the closet door and stepped into the corridor. She was instantly bombarded by streamers, blaring horns, and noisemakers. Shouts and cries quickly followed, and she and

Salem were surrounded by half the student body.

Mr. Kraft's angry voice cut through the din. "Miss Spellman, you have been very irresponsible! You're late for the pep rally!"

The football players pushed through the crowd and surrounded them. Sabrina was glad to see Harvey, but he looked past her and went straight to Salem. "Where have you been?" cooed Harvey.

Salem purred with delight and jumped into Harvey's arms. He comforted the spoiled cat, stroking his matted fur. "What has that bad Sabrina been doing with you?"

"Yeah, Sabrina," said Brad angrily. "You had us really worried. And what were you doing in that closet?"

Mr. Kraft folded his arms and stamped his foot. "If you're not careful, I may give this job to someone else."

39

Before Sabrina could say that was fine with her, Harvey shouted in alarm. "Where is Salem's pillow?"

"You *lost* his silk pillow!" said Brad accusingly.

Sabrina put her hands on her hips and stared back at them. "It was crazy at the pet store—you should have been there!"

"What a pathetic excuse," said Mr. Kraft with disgust. "I'll deal with you later, Miss Spellman. Now that Salem's here, we can start the pep rally!"

Everyone screamed and shouted, and the horns and streamers started up again. Harvey hoisted Salem triumphantly over his head, and the football team surrounded him as he marched into the auditorium. A great roar went up at the sight of Salem, and the cat nodded at his subjects like an emperor.

As the crowd rushed past her, Sa-

brina sighed and slumped against the wall. It was bad enough to be his assistant, but she also had to *live* with him. She didn't think she could survive another day of Salem being the high school mascot.

41

Chapter 5

"Could you flip the newspaper for me, Sabrina?" asked Salem with a yawn. "My paws are tired."

Sabrina looked up from the kitchen table, where she was doing her homework. Salem was sitting on the kitchen counter, wearing his glasses and reading the newspaper. Now the cat read the sports section every day, looking for articles about himself.

Sabrina kept studying. "You can't turn the pages yourself?"

42

"Me?" answered Salem indignantly. "I might get ink on my paws. If my football players were here, *they* would do it for me."

Sabrina rolled her eyes. "You mean your slaves?"

"Well, I try not to call them that." Salem licked his fur and preened for a moment. He finally turned the newspaper himself and began to read.

"Oh, here's a mention of me!" crowed the cat. Salem cleared his throat and read out loud, " 'Westbridge High is the favorite in their game . . . blah-blah-blah. Also on hand will be their new mascot, Salem the black cat. Since the fabulous feline starting running across the paths of opposing teams, the Fighting Scallions have won every game.' "

Salem grinned. "He called me a 'fabulous feline.' I'll have to use that in my ads. Sabrina, will you cut this story out for me? I want to put it with my press clippings."

43

"In a minute," answered Sabrina. "My textbook is more important than your scrapbook."

Salem sniffed. "I don't believe you're showing the proper respect for your mascot."

The teenager sighed. "Salem, I'm really happy that the team is winning. But I haven't seen *you* score a touchdown or make a tackle."

"I inspire the boys," said Salem with a sniff. "Don't forget about the bottom line. We're winning!"

Angrily Salem turned the page, then he arched his back and hissed at the newspaper.

That got Sabrina out of her seat. "What's wrong?"

"It's a big picture of a really hideous dog. It startled me."

"Let me see." Sabrina leaned over her kitty to see the photo of a fat, jowly bull-

dog. He was wearing a sweater and holding a pennant in his paws. She started reading the story, and she smiled.

"Look, Salem! He's a mascot just like you."

"What do you mean, just like me?" asked the cat suspiciously. "You mean other pets are doing this mascot stuff? I thought I had this racket to myself."

"Well, this one is." Sabrina read aloud, "For ten years Old Butch the bulldog has been the mascot at Old Ivy Dominion. Old Butch is sure to be on the field this Saturday when the local college opens conference play against Placidville University."

The teenage witch put down the newspaper and smiled slyly. "He's the mascot at a big college, and you're only the mascot at a high school."

Salem hissed again. "This . . . this . . . *dog* has a better job than I do?"

45

"Sure he does. Their games are on TV, and he gets to travel all over the country."

"I want his job," declared Salem.

Sabrina chuckled, then she stopped laughing. She couldn't tell if the black cat was joking or not. "Old Butch has been at this college for ten years," she said.

"Then they need some new blood," answered Salem. "High school is too limiting for me. Not enough exposure. I've got to branch out into college football. After that, the pros! Then maybe I'll invent my own sport, and I'll be the mascot on every team!"

Now Sabrina was not laughing. "Salem, that's crazy. Just be happy where you are."

The cat begged her, "Please help me! You can pretend to be my agent and talk to the dean at Old Ivy Dominion. We'll bring all my press clippings."

"Why should they change mascots?" asked Sabrina.

"Because my team *wins!*" shouted Salem. "Remember the bottom line. Besides, wouldn't it be great to have me *out* of your school? I'd be causing trouble somewhere else. If you do this for me, Sabrina, I promise to be nicer to you, Hilda, and Zelda."

"In that case," said Sabrina, "I'll call him. I warn you, I'm not using any witchcraft to help you. You'll have to get the job on your own."

She took another look at the photo of the grizzled bulldog. "I wouldn't count on getting this dog's job. He doesn't look like he wants to go anywhere."

"We'll see," answered Salem, swishing his tail.

Chapter 6

Old Ivy Dominion sounded just like its name, thought Sabrina. There was old ivy growing all over old gray bricks, and the buildings looked like forts from the Middle Ages. Salem purred in her arms, obviously pleased.

"This a very dignified campus," said Salem with approval.

"You keep quiet and let me do the talking," insisted Sabrina. She smiled at a group of college students who walked by.

"They're so dignified here, they might not like talking cats."

Salem whispered, "Have you got my scrapbook?"

"Right here." Sabrina patted her briefcase. She was dressed in a dark business suit and looked older than a teenager, she hoped.

"And my video?"

"Yes."

They approached an old building that towered over the others like a cathedral. There was so much ivy crawling all over its walls that she couldn't even see the bricks. The sign said Administration Building, and that was where they had to go.

They walked inside the lobby and were met by a stern-faced receptionist. The walls of the lobby were covered with trophies, pennants, and photos. There was a big framed picture of Old Butch hanging in the middle of the room.

"I'm Sabrina Spellman from the Happy Mascot Talent Agency," she said. "We have a four o'clock appointment with the dean."

The woman checked her appointment book and saw that Sabrina was listed. "Do you have to take the cat in?" she asked.

"That's the whole point of the visit," said Sabrina. "This is Salem, the famous mascot for Westbridge High School."

"I see," said the woman with a sniff. "Of course, he's not as famous as *our* Old Butch."

"Or as ugly," hissed a voice.

"What did you say?" asked the woman suspiciously.

Of course, Sabrina hadn't said it—Salem had. But now she had to cover for the talking cat. She laughed nervously and replied, "I said, 'He's very *snuggly.'*"

"Isn't he, though!" exclaimed the re-

ceptionist. She looked fondly at the picture of Old Butch. "I would just love to snuggle with him, too. You can take the elevator to the third floor. The dean is waiting."

"Thank you." Gripping Salem and her briefcase, Sabrina hurried into the elevator.

As soon as the elevator door closed, Salem snarled. "When I'm the mascot here, I'm going to have that woman fired."

Sabrina frowned. "Remember, *I* do the talking. You're just the talent, so keep quiet."

"Okay," sniffed Salem. "I'll just flash him my charisma."

When the elevator door opened, they were met by a portly man in a three-piece suit. "Welcome, Miss Spellman. I'm Dean Franklin. Is this cute kitty the Salem I've heard so much about?"

The black cat purred and batted his

eyes at the dean. "Yes, it is," answered Sabrina. "He's been doing great as the mascot for Westbridge High. They haven't lost a game since he started."

"That is impressive," agreed Dean Franklin. "Come into my office."

The dean escorted them into a beautiful office with rich wood paneling and antique furnishings. Sabrina dropped Salem into a plush armchair, and he stretched his legs and claws. Salem always liked expensive, old furniture, and Sabrina could tell he liked it here.

Dean Franklin sat at his desk and folded his hands. "Tell me about your client."

Sabrina fumbled in her briefcase for Salem's scrapbook. "Why don't I show you all his clippings? He's gotten a lot of great publicity."

"Fine." The dean took the scrapbook from her and skimmed the articles. Sa-

brina glanced over at Salem, who curled his tail happily. He loved to watch someone reading about how wonderful he was.

"Very impressive," said Dean Franklin. "What sort of show does Salem put on?"

"Well, he always runs in front of the opposing team. You know, it's bad luck for a black cat to cross your path. Then the cheerleaders carry him around on a pillow. Sometimes he rolls around in the grass." Sabrina looked in her briefcase. "I have a video here—"

The dean held up his hand. "That's all right, Miss Spellman. I'm impressed with Salem, but I think we'll stick with the dog."

"But that Old Butch must be old," said Sabrina. "What happens if he . . . you know . . . goes to the big kennel in the sky?"

"Let me show you something," said the

dean. He opened up a desk drawer and took out a stack of photos. Then he spread the photos on his desk so Sabrina could see them.

Some of the photos were really old, in black-and-white, but all of them were pictures of bulldogs. Some of the bulldogs were young, some were old, but they were all wearing the same red sweater. "I don't get it," said Sabrina, puzzled.

The dean smiled. "There have been eighteen dogs named Old Butch, going back 180 years to our first wrestling team. When one gets too old, we just get another bulldog. So we will always have an Old Butch."

"Wow!" said Sabrina. "Talk about job security."

"I'd like to make a change, but I don't think the fans would let me get rid of Old Butch." The dean stood up and shook

Sabrina's hand. "Thank you for coming, Miss Spellman. You, too, Salem. I'm sorry things won't work out."

A minute later Sabrina and Salem were riding down in the elevator. Salem grumbled, "Why didn't you tell them I'm a warlock and won't get as old as a real cat? They wouldn't have to get a new Salem every ten years!"

Sabrina rolled her eyes. "You know what happens if you tell a mortal you're a witch. That is, unless you really want to turn into a mouse."

"Okay, okay!" snapped the cat. "I guess there are other colleges."

Sabrina and Salem left the administration building and walked across the lawn between the ivy-covered buildings. They were strolling down a tree-lined sidewalk when they saw a crowd of students coming toward them.

Sabrina picked Salem up and watched

in amazement. The crowd was led by cheerleaders, who did cartwheels all along the way. They were followed by a bunch of muscular male cheerleaders carrying a litter. The litter was like a huge dog house on poles, and inside the house was a fat old bulldog. He was wearing a sweater and sitting on a purple throne.

Old Butch, thought Sabrina.

This grand procession made Salem's pillow look like a rag. The cat tensed in her arms, and she knew he was getting mad. As the parade passed by, Old Butch looked down at them and sneered. It was clear that the dog thought the cat was way beneath him.

"Grrrr," grumbled Salem. He squirmed in Sabrina's arms, but she held him tightly. With cheerleaders and students yelling cheers, the happy crowd moved off.

"Hmmm," said Sabrina. "It does look like a nice job for a pet."

"No kidding," said Salem. "College is the place to be. I've got to get that job!"

"Forget it, Salem," said the teenager. "They already told us they weren't hiring a new mascot. This job belongs to Old Butch Eighteen, and then Old Butch Nineteen."

"We'll see about that," vowed Salem.

Chapter 7

Salem strolled into the living room just as the doorbell rang. It was Friday night, and another big game for Westbridge High. Sabrina rushed down the stairs to open the door, and she was happy to be greeted by Harvey's smiling face.

"Harvey!" she exclaimed. "I wasn't expecting you to pick me up!"

"Actually, I've come to pick up Salem." Harvey gave her a sheepish grin, then looked past her. His eyes lit up when he saw Salem. "Come here, boy!"

Salem waltzed slowly toward Harvey, and he looked pathetically at Sabrina. She just pouted and said, "I'll see Your Highness at the game."

Salem wanted to remind her not to forget the picnic basket, but he couldn't talk with Harvey around. The boy and the black cat walked across the lawn to Harvey's car. Harvey was just about to open the door for Salem when a teenage boy on crutches limped by. His leg was in a cast.

"There he is!" shouted the student on crutches. He waggled his finger at Salem. "That's the cat who broke my leg and made me lose my job! That's right, Salem—I'm the mascot you put out of business. I'm the Dancing Scallion!"

"Come on, Vince," said Harvey, trying to shield Salem from the angry guy on crutches. "*You* only wanted to be a mascot to get close to the cheerleaders.

Salem is just a cat—he doesn't scheme and plan like that. Besides, this is show business. One day you're a scallion, and the next day you're nobody."

Excuse me, thought Salem, *they don't pay you for this job, and you have to wear a vegetable costume. You should be* thanking *me!*

But Vince glared at Salem. "You mark my words, cat—someday *you'll* take the fall. You'll be riding high, and then you'll be out on your tail!"

Not me, thought Salem. *In fact, fellow mascot, you've given me a great idea.*

Harvey quickly opened the car door. "Get in, Salem."

He kept a close watch on the angry student until the cat was safely in the car. After Harvey jumped in and started the engine, he muttered. "How rude. I hope he didn't scare you, Salem. Although I do feel kind of sorry for him."

Salem shrugged and settled down on the backseat. He was glad he had run into the old mascot. Now he knew how he was going to get the bulldog's job—exactly the same way.

The whistles sounded, and the referees waved their hands. "The game is over!" declared the announcer. "The Fighting Scallions hold on to defeat the Bellevue Bear Cubs by a score of fourteen to thirteen!"

A cheerleader grabbed Salem and swung him around, and everybody jumped and cheered. Salem breathed a sigh of relief because they had barely won the game. Only a last-minute touchdown had saved them from defeat.

But his unbeaten record was intact. That was good, because Salem wanted to go out a winner. If everything went as planned, this would be his last game for Westbridge High School.

The football players crowded around him, petting and hugging him. But Salem was more interested in the visiting team than the Fighting Scallions. He heard somebody say the Bear Cubs were from a nearby town, close to Old Ivy Dominion. That was where he wanted to go.

Salem winked at Sabrina and pointed his tail toward the bleachers. They slipped away from the happy crowd and gathered in the dark shadows at the back of the seats.

"I'll go home by myself," said Salem. "You take some time off and be with Harvey."

"Really?" asked Sabrina in amazement. "Are you sure you can get home?"

"No problem," answered Salem. "I've got lots of fans around here, including one who owns a sleek Siamese named Linda Lu."

"Salem, you old rascal." Sabrina glared at her familiar for a moment, then her face broke into a smile. "Thanks a lot. Gotta go!"

As soon as Sabrina was out of sight, Salem dashed under the bleachers and ran into the parking lot. He looked for the team bus and found it quickly because of all the signs and banners. The bus was empty because the visiting players were still in the locker room. There was a bus driver, but he wasn't paying much attention.

Salem crouched in the shadows until the driver opened the door and walked away. Then he dashed onto the bus and found a hiding place under a seat in the back. He curled up into a little ball, so small no one would notice. He was going to get a nice ride to the next town . . . and Old Ivy Dominion.

Tomorrow was going to be the college's

big game, and Salem intended to be the star.

"That's odd," said Sabrina the next morning. "I don't think Salem came home last night."

"Oh, he was probably out celebrating," answered Dreama. The young witch stretched out on the couch in the living room. "Maybe his fans took him home."

"Yeah, that's possible," admitted Sabrina. "We don't see much of Salem since he's become a celebrity."

"Doesn't Harvey usually bring him home?" asked Dreama.

"Usually," answered Sabrina. "But he didn't last night, because he actually went out with *me* for a change. Salem said he had another way home."

"I'm sure he's okay," said Dreama. "Has he ever stayed out all night before?"

"Yeah," answered Sabrina, feeling foolish.

Dreama snapped her fingers. "If you want, you could do a finder spell, but you need a troll for that."

"And I'm fresh out of trolls," said Sabrina. "All right, I'll wait until tonight and see if he shows up." The teenage witch crossed her arms and looked out the window. "I wonder where Salem Saberhagen could be?"

Salem poked his head out of the garbage can, where he had spent the night eating and sleeping. In the distance he could hear a marching band playing. It was Saturday afternoon—time for the big game at Old Ivy Dominion.

The cat jumped out of the garbage can and shook a banana peel off his back. Maybe he smelled a little ripe, but so what? He still had that Salem charisma.

65

He just followed the crowds and the music to the stadium. This was no high-school stadium—this was a football palace about ten stories high. People were streaming into the stadium, and it was filling rapidly. There had to be sixty or seventy thousand people!

I haven't seen this many people in one place since the Romans shut down the Colosseum, thought Salem.

The cat crept around to the back and squirmed under a gate. He slipped through the parking lot, which was filled with big white trucks. Thick black cables snaked all over the ground.

Of course, thought Salem. *It's the TV crew! This is the big time. Today* The Salem Show *goes on national TV!*

The happy cat made sure to pass by the director's truck, just to make sure everything was okay. He crouched under the door and listened.

"It's a beautiful day for football," droned the TV announcer's voice. "The teams are just about to take the field. But first . . . here comes Old Butch, the beloved mascot of Old Ivy Dominion. The cheerleaders are bringing him in on his luxury litter. I tell you, folks, *that* is the only way to travel!"

I'll have you *fired, too*, thought Salem.

"They're setting Old Butch down beside his private fire hydrant," said the announcer. "And look, he has a little stuffed cat to rip apart whenever Old Ivy scores a touchdown!"

"Grrrr," growled Salem. *It's time to dethrone this stupid dog and take his job!*

He looked around and spotted some metal bleachers near the end zone. That would be a perfect place to hide. Besides, he always started his act from the bleach-

ers. The marching band struck up a lively tune, and the crowd cheered.

"It's show time!" said Salem. With dreams of fame dancing in his head, the black cat dashed into the football stadium.

Chapter 8

Salem hid under the bleachers, with lots of other garbage. He figured he must really be smelly now, but he still had his charm. The cat was able to watch the game and enjoy it . . . until Old Ivy Dominion scored their first touchdown.

That was when Old Butch did his act. Because Old Butch was near the end zone, right in front of Salem, the cat could see him perfectly. A cheerleader held out a toy stuffed cat, and the old bulldog jumped up and ripped it to

pieces. The crowd cheered louder than they had for the touchdown.

That was when Salem lost it. He couldn't help himself. The black cat shot out from under the bleachers, and he ran right past Old Butch. The bulldog blinked as if he didn't believe it, then his body went stiff as a board. He whirled around, barking like a maniac. On his stubby legs Old Butch took off after the streaking cat.

This surprised Salem, because he thought that the dog was tied down. Shouldn't all dogs be tied down? This forced him to run out of bounds, where the marching band was standing. Just as he had done at Westbridge High, Salem ran between their legs and made the tuba players and drummers crash into each other.

Only this time the audience didn't find it funny. At least, they didn't laugh.

Instead most of them screamed, "Get him, Butch! Get that cat! Tackle him!"

Salem heard a growl. He whirled around and saw the crazed bulldog headed right toward him. His jaws were dripping with foam and drool, and his beady eyes bugged out. Salem jumped over a short fence into the stands. Old Butch tried to stop in time, but he crashed headfirst into the fence.

"Oooooh!" roared the seventy thousand people at once.

Salem ran along the bench seats in the stands, making everyone jump up and scream. Once again they weren't laughing. In fact, most of them threw their purses and drinks at Salem as he ran past. "Pull his tail!" shouted one lady.

This isn't working out like I planned! thought Salem desperately. He ran down the middle aisle and jumped over the fence again. This time he landed on top

of a TV cameraman, who screamed and whirled around. His big video camera hit Salem like a baseball bat and swatted the cat into the middle of the field.

Salem landed on his back and rolled over. He sat up in a daze. When his vision cleared, he saw about fifty police officers and football officials charging toward him. Then he heard a horrible howl, and he saw Old Butch coming from the other direction. The dog's squished, ugly face looked even uglier after running into the fence.

"Uh-oh!" shouted Salem. He jumped high in the air just as the crowd ran into Old Butch, causing a major pileup. Salem scrambled down the back of one of the policemen and dashed for the bleachers.

"Get him!" shouted the fans. "Get that cat!"

When he got close to the bleachers, about a hundred people rose out of their

seats to stop him. It seemed as if everybody in the stadium was chasing him, including the football players!

"Help!" screamed the cat.

Sabrina was pacing in her living room, wondering where Salem was. It was still daylight outside, and she knew she shouldn't be worried. But Salem had been acting awfully funny lately. What if he had been catnapped?

With nothing else to do, Sabrina decided to watch some television. She turned on the TV, and of course it was a football game. That was all Salem watched anymore, and every TV in the house was tuned to football night and day.

This was a funny game, because it looked as if more people were playing than usual. In fact, everyone in the stadium seemed to be running around on the field. They were chasing something,

but it was small and difficult to see. She turned up the volume.

"If black cats are bad luck," said the TV announcer, "then we're all in for bad luck. That black cat has crossed the path of at least ten thousand people. And he's still running!"

"Maybe they should sign that cat up for fullback," said the other announcer with a laugh.

"I don't think there will be much left of him after Old Butch gets to him," said the first announcer.

Sabrina sat forward and stared at the TV. The screen showed a close-up of a terrified black cat with a bulldog and hundreds of people chasing it. They were going to tear the kitty apart!

Oh, my gosh! thought Sabrina. *It's Salem!*

The teenage witch jumped to her feet and twirled her finger in the air. "I have

to catch him before *they* do. Or Salem will be kitty stew!"

She snapped her fingers, and she was suddenly Sabrina, animal control specialist. She was wearing a pith helmet and brown uniform. With a cage in one hand and a net in the other, she looked very official. Satisfied with her appearance, Sabrina nodded her head. She disappeared in a sparkling blast of magic.

People were closing in from all sides, and a bulldog snapped at his tail. Salem was desperate when he saw the tunnel entrance off to his right. He didn't even know where it went. Running and panting, the black cat plunged down the ramp into the darkened tunnel.

He got about halfway down when he knew he was in big trouble. This hallway led to the locker room, and there was no other way out. With a mob of crazy peo-

ple and a nasty dog chasing him, Salem cut to his right and ducked through a swinging door.

Now he was really in the locker room, and it was steamy from someone using the shower. He dashed between rows of lockers, and his pursuers spread out to find him. They closed off every exit, and he had nowhere to go. As strange hands reached for him, Salem leaped on top of the lockers.

He ran along the top of the lockers until he got to the end. Then he flew off and landed in the shower. He hated to get wet, but maybe he could lose them in the steam and hot water.

But the stadium workers and police officers followed him right into the showers. A TV camera crew charged after them, trying to get the cat on video.

This strange parade ran past two athletes who were taking showers, and they

ducked out of sight. Old Butch charged through the water and stepped on a bar of soap. The dog skidded about twenty feet, hit the ledge, and took off flying. He landed in a laundry bag.

There were just too many people, and the locker room was too small. Salem ran as far as he could, but he got trapped in a corner. The cat whirled around and saw a wall of angry people moving in. He hissed at them and arched his back, but they just kept coming.

It looked like the end for Salem.

Chapter 9

"Let me through! Let me through!" bellowed a voice. "I'm with Animal Control, and that feline is *mine!* We'll teach him to break the laws."

Salem was cowering in the corner, surrounded by dozens of people eager to catch him. A blond dogcatcher with a cage and a net pushed her way through the crowd. Salem was about ready to make another break for it, when he took a good look at the woman.

It's Sabrina!

She put the cage on the floor and motioned at him with the net. "Now, you get in here, you bad kitty!"

Salem never moved so fast to do as he was told. He dashed into the cage, and Sabrina slammed it tight and locked it. "Yes, he's a ferocious one," she said. "And smelly, too."

"Where are you taking him?" asked a burly policeman.

Sabrina tried to squeeze past the officer. "Um, we're taking him downtown. We'll book him, and then we'll *throw* the book at him. Playing football without a license!"

Suddenly she bumped into a large man in a suit. It was Dean Franklin, and he glared at her. "You're not from Animal Control—you're his *agent!* This is all a publicity stunt!"

"Uh-oh!" Sabrina made a mad dash for the door, and she escaped from the

locker room before anybody could catch her. She ran down the hallway, carrying the net and the cage. A policeman blew his whistle, and the crowd chased after her.

Sabrina threw the net over her shoulder, and it dropped on the first three officers. They fell down in a heap, and everyone tumbled over them, blocking the hallway. Sabrina and Salem were able to get outside and run to the parking lot.

"Oh, thank you, thank you!" gushed Salem. "I'll never try to be a college mascot again. I'll be happy at Westbridge High."

"Forget it," snapped Sabrina. "Your mascot days are over!" She ran behind a big white TV truck. When she was sure nobody could see them, she twirled her finger in the air. They disappeared in a poof of sparkling confetti.

*   *   *

Weeks later the Westbridge football team was still winning most of its games, even without Salem. No matter how much Harvey and his teammates begged to get Salem back, Sabrina stood firm. His mascot days were over.

The black cat begged Sabrina to take him back to Westbridge High to see a game. Couldn't he at least *watch* football? Sabrina felt sort of guilty. If she had just taken Salem to a football game to begin with, none of this would have happened.

So one Friday night she took Salem to a football game. Some people recognized the black cat, and they waved to him in the stands. The dancing scallion guy was back, although he still looked silly in his vegetable costume.

"Do you think they've forgotten about me?" whispered Salem. "They seem to like the vegetable dude."

"Of course they remember you," said

Sabrina. "Now sit back and enjoy the game."

At halftime the dancing scallion changed his costume. In the second half of the game, he was dressed like a black cat. He rolled around on the grass and ran in front of the visiting team, just like Salem used to. The crowd cheered its approval.

The cat was so happy, he began to cry. "They *do* remember me!"

Sabrina rolled her eyes. "Salem, nobody could ever forget you."

Cat Care Tips

1. Cats should always have fresh food available, since they like to eat frequently throughout the day and night. Cats should eat a good, well-known brand of cat food, since they have very specific nutritional needs. It is fine for them to have snacks of human food if you want to indulge them, but their main diet should always be cat food.

2. Make sure the cat food you use says that it is completely nutritionally balanced for cats. Try to vary the flavors that your cat receives (unless you have specific instructions from your veterinarian). Cats should not have tuna fish flavor too often.

3. Never, never let your cat go on a food fast—if he or she does not eat the type of food that you are giving within twenty-four hours you must try another flavor or type of food. Cats will not eat food that they do not like no mat-

ter how hungry they get, and they can get very sick if they don't eat for as few as three days. Cats **do not** follow the rule that when they get hungry enough they will eat whatever food you have selected.

—Laura E. Smiley, MS, DVM, Dipl. ACVIM
Gwynedd Veterinary Hospital

Sabrina

The Teenage Witch®

Salem's Tails®

What's it like to be a powerful warlock,
sentenced to one hundred years in a
cat's body for trying to take over the world?

Ask Salem.

**Read all about Salem's magical
adventures in this series based on the hit
ABC-TV show!**

A MINSTREL® BOOK
Published by Pocket Books

2007-12

EASY TO READ—FUN TO SOLVE!

Meet up with suspense and mystery in The Hardy Boys® are:

THE CLUES™ BROTHERS

Available from Minstrel® Books
Published by Pocket Books

2389

BILL W

Award-winning author B   d
animal stories full of humor and exciting adventures.

BEAUTY

RED DOG*

TRAPPED IN DEATH CAVE*

A DOG CALLED KITTY

DANGER ON PANTHER PEAK

SNOT STEW

**FERRET IN THE BEDROOM,
LIZARDS IN THE FRIDGE**

DANGER IN QUICKSAND SWAMP

THE CHRISTMAS SPURS

TOTALLY DISGUSTING!

BUFFALO GAL

NEVER SAY QUIT

BIGGEST KLUTZ IN FIFTH GRADE

BLACKWATER SWAMP

WATCHDOG AND THE COYOTES

TRUE FRIENDS

JOURNEY INTO TERROR

THE FINAL FREEDOM

THE BACKWARD BIRD DOG

UPCHUCK AND THE ROTTEN WILLY

**UPCHUCK AND THE ROTTEN WILLY:
THE GREAT ESCAPE**

THE FLYING FLEA, CALLIE, AND ME

ALOHA SUMMER

**UPCHUCK AND THE ROTTEN WILLY:
RUNNING WILD**

A MINSTREL® BOOK
Published by Pocket Books

*Available from Archway Paperbacks

648-31